Janet Lawler

LOVE IS REAL

illustrations by
Anna Brown

HARPER
An Imprint of HarperCollinsPublishers

Library of Congress Cataloging-in-Publication Data is available.
ISBN 978-0-06-224170-2 (trade bdg.)

The artist used a variety of textured and colored papers and Photoshop
to create the digital collaged illustrations for this book.
Typography by Martha Rago
13 14 15 16 17   SCP   10 9 8 7 6 5 4 3 2 1
❖
First Edition

To Mary S.—who has lived my words

—J.L.

For Ma and Pa Brown

—A.B.

Love is in the little things

that fill my heart until it sings.

Love awakes

and helps you dress.

Love will clean up any mess.

Love keeps droopy laces tied

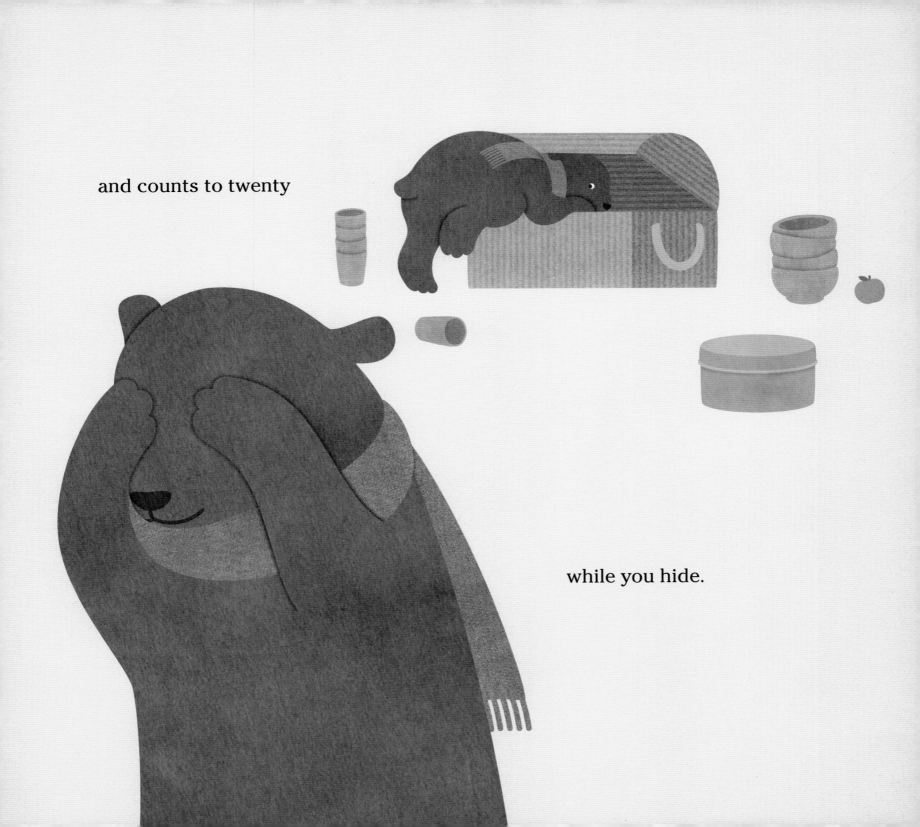

and counts to twenty

while you hide.

Love holds on to steer your bike

and packs a picnic lunch you like.

Love throws gently to your glove

and frees the kite that's stuck above.

Love can be a silly clown
who makes you smile
instead of frown.

Love puts sprinkles on the top.

Love can dance
the bunny hop.

Love
will
help
you
climb
a
tree

and tape a bandage to your knee.

Love serves apples, sliced up thin,

and finds a game that you can win.

Love creates a castle moat

and salvages a sinking boat.

Love will listen
when you tug.

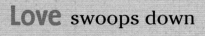

Love swoops down
to give a hug.

Love plays lion

in a crouch

and snuggles closer
on the couch.

Love unknots

your tangled hair

and finds a special book to share.

Love does all
these little things
to fill your heart
until it sings.

Love is real the whole day through.

It's always there—

from me to you.